COLLECTION MANAGEMENT

7/9/14	8—	1/10/11

The Adventures of Hector Fuller

BOOK 2

Hector Finds a Fortune

The Adventures of Hector Fuller

BOOK 2

Hector Finds a Fortune

By Elizabeth Shreeve
Illustrated by Pamela Levy

ALADDIN
New York London Toronto Sydney

To Dr. Walton Daddy-O Shreeve —E. S.

First Aladdin Library edition January 2004

Text copyright © 2004 by Elizabeth Shreeve
Illustrations copyright © 2004 by Pamela Levy

ALADDIN PAPERBACKS
An imprint of Simon & Schuster
Children's Publishing Division
1230 Avenue of the Americas
New York, NY 10020

Also available in an Aladdin Paperback edition

Designed by Debra Sfetsios
The text of this book was set in Graham.

Printed in the United States of America
2 4 6 8 10 9 7 5 3 1

Library of Congress Control Number 2003106062
ISBN 0-689-86419-1

BOOK 2

Hector Finds
a Fortune

Table of Contents

Chapter One

Opportunity Knocks

On a summer day a letter came to the home of Hector Fuller the wumblebug. Hector hardly ever got mail, so his friends crowded around as he checked the address: HECTOR FULLER, WUMBLEBUG HOLE, GARDENSIDE.

That was Hector, all right—six legs, four short wings, and a cozy cave for all a bug could want.

"Aren't you going to open it?" asked Lance the lacewing, Hector's best friend. The bugs were playing cards and drinking mint tea in Hector's kitchen, sheltered from the midday sun.

Hector opened the envelope and pulled out the letter. His antennae shivered as he read aloud:

"Dear Hector,

You may wonder why I am writing to you after all this time. Well, you might remember that I have a large business up here. It's too much work for me now, and I want to see if you can help. Follow the stream up . . . and you won't get lost.

> Uncle Baxter
> Baxter's Bee Farm
> The Meadow."

Hector stared at the words. He read them over and over to himself, until he could almost hear old Uncle Baxter himself.

"When will you go?" Lance's voice made Hector jump.

"Go? Do you think I should go?"

"Sure," Lance said. "Why not?"

"Well, for one thing, it's a long way. Second, I'm not sure if I want to work on a bee farm. All that buzzing . . . kind of gives me the creeps."

Hector tried to swallow, but his throat felt dry. "Third, it's nice and cool down here, and it's hot outside, and—"

"You should give it a try," said Suzy, the plump and lovely ladybug who was Hector's favorite cousin. "He's your uncle, after all."

"Not only that," said Lance, "he owns the biggest bee farm around. You'd never have to worry about finding enough food. Even in a year like this."

"That's true." Hector looked at his empty kitchen. "But still . . ."

"Hector, you're impossible." Lance jumped up and scattered the deck of cards all over the floor. "C'mon, we'll leave right now."

Hector's jaw dropped open. "You'll come with me?"

"Do you think I'd let you go alone?" Lance's long wings shimmered and shook. "After all, there's nothing much to eat around here. Hand me your pack—we'll bring those last two blue-berries. And a mint leaf, for tea."

"That's the last of the food," said Hector.

"We'll have to find some more along the way."

The friends hurried to get ready, not knowing what they would find on the journey ahead.

Chapter Two

Senior Citizen

Outside, Hector and Lance breathed the good, clean smell of dust and grass stems baking in the sun. The summer weather had been dry. Every morning arrived with a clear sky, then clouds gathered and thunder rumbled in the distance. But no rain came to break the heat.

The two travelers found the stream, shaded by an arching tunnel of willow trees. After the dry weather the water was just a trickle, and the bugs could hop from rock to rock as they made their way uphill. Lance threw himself into the air, flapping and flopping his long wings. Soon he was far ahead.

Hector lagged behind. His legs felt heavier with every step.

He stopped and looked back. Below him the stony streambed was quiet except for one flicker of movement—a leaf that was climbing up the stream, all by itself.

The leaf stopped just below Hector at a spot where the streambed rose in a small cliff. A face popped out. It was a little old termite lady, holding the leaf as a sunshade as she hiked along.

Hector reached down the cliff. "Here," he said. "Can I help you up?"

"No . . . thank you, . . . my dear," said the termite lady, puffing and panting. "Keeps me . . . fit as a fiddle. One step . . . at a time. As they say,"—she plopped down next to Hector and fanned herself with the leaf—"haste makes waste!"

"Are you traveling up to the meadow?" asked Hector.

She shook her head. "Daughter's had more babies. Going to help. That's the long and short of it! This trip is just the calm before the storm."

"Is there a storm coming?"

The termite lady chuckled. "Thunder at night,

traveler's delight. Thunder in the morning, all the day storming. You'll need to remember that if you're traveling as far as the meadow. Are you alone?"

"No. My friend Lance is up ahead. He's a lacewing."

"Two heads are better than one! Remember well and bear in mind, a true friend is hard to find! But you'll need to keep your eyes peeled for that friend of yours. Lacewings think they can fly. Long wings. Can't, though. He'll need some looking after."

"More like the other way around," said Hector. "Lance is a lot bigger than I am. And braver, too."

"Now, a wumblebug is a sensible creature," said the termite lady as if she hadn't heard. "Feet on the ground. Nose to the wind. What takes you to the meadow?"

"My uncle's got a bee farm there, and—"

"A farmer is as busy as a bee!"

"Huh? Well, that's why I'm going. He wants me to help him out. But I don't really like bees.

And I don't know if I want to live up there without my friends, and besides—"

"Nothing ventured, nothing gained!"

"I mean, I want to help and everything," said Hector. "But—"

"A bug of words and not of deeds is like a garden full of weeds. Once you get started, it will be as easy as falling off a log. Now, here you go, wumblebug." She stood up and pulled a smooth white pebble out of her bag. "You see the stripe that goes all the way around? It's good luck."

"Thank you," said Hector. "I'll keep it with me."

"And don't forget," she said as she took a path leading away from the stream. "Think of a fly, think of a flea. When something tickles you, think of me!"

The termite lady waved her leaf one last time and disappeared from sight.

Chapter Three

Whirligigs

Hector rubbed the smooth pebble and tucked it into his pack. There was the letter. He pulled it out and read it again.

The termite lady made things sound easy. But what if Hector didn't get along with the bees? What if his uncle wanted him to stay, and he never saw his home again?

It would be simple to write a letter back.

> *Dear Uncle Baxter,*
>   *It was wonderful to hear from you. . . .*

No. That wasn't really true.

Dear Uncle Baxter,
   Due to current obligations, I will not be . . .

No. That was worse.

Dear Uncle Baxter,
   Forget it. Why would I want to live with a bunch of bees?

Lance would like that one.

Hector laughed and started up the stream again. He rounded a bend, looked up, and stopped dead in his tracks.

Just ahead the stream tumbled in a noisy waterfall to a pool. At the foot of the waterfall was Lance, dancing on a mossy rock. All around him a crowd of whirligig beetles giggled and cheered, showing off their special talent for gliding across the surface of the water. They skittered in circles and dived and spun, clapping for Lance at the same time.

"Ooh! Look-ee look!" squealed one of the

whirligigs. "Too cute! Hee-hee-hee!"

"Dance with him!" squeaked another. "Dance with the lacewing!"

"No, no, not me!" The first whirligig darted around in a flash of silver and black. "You do it! Hee-hee!"

"You! You! You said he was cute!" Two or three others joined in the chorus.

"Dance with a lacewing? Eeuuuww! Never!"

Lance grinned at Hector and turned a full circle on the slippery rock. But Lance did not see what Hector saw—a fat raccoon at the top of the waterfall. She dipped her hands in the shallow water and cracked open a nut. Then she held the nutshell over the edge and stared at Lance with her black eyes.

"Lance, watch out!" Hector's words drowned in the noisy stream. He waved and pointed. Too late. The shell hit the rock. Lance shot into the waterfall and into the swirling water below.

The whirligigs burst into laughter.

"So much for the lacewing!" they shouted. "Hee-hee!"

Hector threw off his pack, jumped in the pool,

and sank. He could see Lance, stuck in the frothy whirlpool. And there was the nutshell, bouncing on the surface. Hector lunged for it and grabbed. Kicking with his back legs, he charged toward Lance and clamped on to his long, wet wings. Then with a great push, Hector broke free of the current and pulled them both up on a rock.

The whirligigs had forgotten Lance. "A ride! A ride!" they chanted at the raccoon. "Goody goody, give us a ride!"

The raccoon scooped a handful of whirligigs out of the water. She lifted them to her mouth and then, one by one, spit them out. Shiny black bodies flew this way and that, shrieking as they sailed through the air and splashed into the pool.

"Whoopee!"

"Whoa!"

The raccoon looked down at Hector and spit one last time. "Eee-ha!" the whirligig cried, and hit Hector full blast, sending him back into the pool.

Hector's head spun. He could not feel or breathe. As if in a dream, he looked up and saw Lance dive in after him. His friend caught his legs and they both sank. Two bugs. Two heads. He remembered—two heads are better than one. He remembered to kick. Lance kicked. Together they kicked against the current and struggled up onto land.

The raccoon was gone. The whirligigs were a distant shadow, spinning away down the stream.

"What were you doing with those stupid bugs?" asked Hector.

Lance shook his head and coughed. "They seemed really friendly at first. But they only wanted to fool around."

"Someday this might seem funny." Hector poked Lance with his elbow. "Don't you think?"

Lance shuddered as lightning shot across the sky. "I think . . . I think I hate thunder," he said. "And rain. There are bats around too. I feel it in my wings."

"I'll make a shelter." Hector got up and walked to the stream. There was the nutshell, washed up on the shore. It would make a good bed. But by the time he dragged it up the bank, Lance was sound asleep.

Chapter Four

Night Lights

Hector dug the nutshell into the beach to make a roof over Lance's head. He piled up sand to keep any waves away. Then he sat and listened to Lance snoring and the stream flowing by. He did not feel sleepy at all.

Thick clouds covered the moon, and the night was dark. Crickets chirped from all directions, and fireflies danced in the air, bringing the stars close. Hector tilted his head back and watched them zig and zag until he was dizzy. At the edge of the woods he saw one speck of light that did not move or blink. He walked up the beach to find it.

In a small clearing was a table spread with a smooth green leaf. On one side sat a brown field cricket. On the other was a firefly who lit the table with her soft, yellow green glow. The two bugs sipped from buttercups and nibbled at salads of watercress. They gazed at each other and sighed.

"Ahem," said Hector, clearing his throat. "Beautiful evening, isn't it?"

The cricket glanced at the wumblebug. "Beautiful," he said.

"Noisy, too," said Hector. "Do crickets chirp faster on a hot night?"

"Of course." The cricket smiled at the firefly. "The hotter it is, the more important to find a friend!"

"Indeed," said the firefly. "Who wants to be lonely on a night like this?"

"No one. Especially if he can be with someone as lovely as you," crooned the cricket, still smiling at her. Then he looked at Hector and his long antennae drooped. "Now, did you . . . would you like to sit down or something?"

Hector looked at the small table set for two. He shook his head. "Thanks. But as a friend of mine might say—two is company, and . . ."

"And?" said the firefly.

"And three is a crowd," said Hector. "I'll be on my way."

The night was darker and cooler now. All the fireflies had found one another, or had given up and gone to bed. Hector made his way back to the beach and lay down near Lance. In a moment he was asleep, and in his dreams the rippling song of the stream became the buzzing sound of bees.

Chapter Five

Honeysuckle

Hector woke to the smell of honeysuckle.

"Thought we'd save the blueberries, so I found these," Lance said, and dropped an armful of blossoms on the sand.

"Thanks." Hector picked up a flower and settled down next to Lance, who was dangling his feet in the stream. The air was already heavy and hot.

Hector cut the bottom off the honeysuckle flower and drank the nectar. It was sweet like honey. "Lance, I've been thinking about the bee farm. I'm not so sure about all this."

"Are you kidding? Baxter's honey is a big business. You see it everywhere!"

"Yeah, but I'd be up there at the meadow all

the time. I don't mind working. It's just so far from home. And you guys. Anyway, I remember my uncle as . . . different. Serious."

"Serious about what?" Lance squinted up as thunder rumbled far away.

"Well, he's not a bad bug or anything. But he's been up there for a long time with bees—who talk a lot, but always about the same things. You know—where's the nectar, how's the queen. He's rich, but he's not very friendly."

"Why's that? You're friendly."

"Of course. But my uncle . . . he's not like me that way."

"Hector, you worry too much. Let's get started before it gets any hotter, okay?" Without waiting for Hector to finish his breakfast, Lance jumped up and flew away up the stream.

Chapter Six

Membership Closed

Hector scrambled to catch up as thunder rumbled again. What had the termite lady said? Something about thunder . . . thunder in the morning. He needed to find Lance.

But Lance was nowhere to be seen. Hector came to a fork, where the stream split in two different directions. As he hopped across the water he could hear voices arguing. Then he saw three figures gathered in a circle on the bank. One was a click beetle, another was a stinkbug, and the third was a roly-poly.

"You're my best friend today," said the roly-poly in a squeaky voice to the stinkbug.

"No, she's *my* best friend." The click beetle waved his stripy wings.

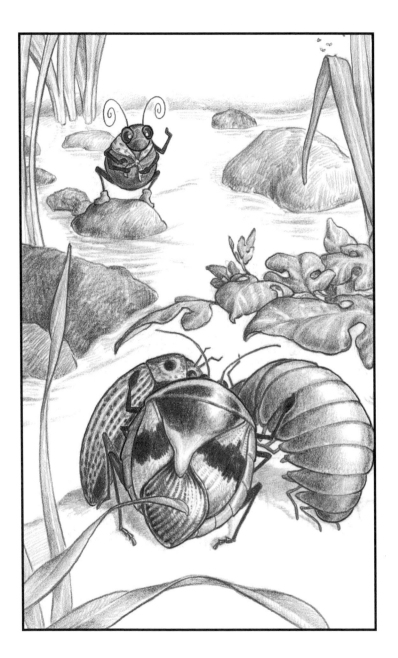

"You were best friends yesterday. It's my turn!" The roly-poly shook her antennae and some of her many legs.

"I don't want to be best friends with either of you," said the stinkbug. "I'm going to make a new club, with somebody you don't even know. So there!"

"Excuse me," said Hector. "Did you see a lacewing go by?"

As soon as he spoke, the three turned their backs to Hector and huddled under a low branch. They giggled, and whispered so he could not hear.

Hector waited, shifting from foot to foot. "Do you happen to know," he said, "which way leads to the meadow?"

Finally the stinkbug looked up and said, "Of course we know. But we only talk to people who know the secret password."

"How do I learn that?" asked Hector.

"Can't!" said the roly-poly. "You have to be part of the club."

"Can I join your club?"

"No! Ha-ha!" said the click beetle, leaning

against the branch. "We have to vote on new members, but we only do that . . ."

"Once a year!" said the roly-poly. "Right?"

"I can't wait that long," said Hector. "I've got to find my friend and get to my uncle's bee farm."

"Oooh," said the stinkbug. "Did you say bee, as in . . . honey? Who is this uncle of yours?"

"His name is Baxter. Maybe you've heard of—"

"Maybe we could make an exception," said the click beetle. "That is, if you're talking about Baxter's Bees."

"Just this once. A special exception. If you've got honey, you can join the club," said the roly-poly.

"Hey, not fair! How come you let him in and not me?" said a voice. It came from the branch— or rather, from a praying mantis that looked like a branch. Her long green body towered over their heads.

The group burst apart. The click beetle catapulted backward with a loud *snap*. The stinkbug let loose with a terrible-smelling spray and scurried into the woods. And the roly-poly curled up in a ball and rolled out of sight down the bank.

Chapter Seven

Life Is Not Fair

"I hate when they do that!" said the praying mantis. For such a tall bug, her voice was high and shrill. "They're always afraid I'll eat them. That's the trouble."

Hector coughed and waved his wings to chase away the stinkbug's terrible smell. "Well, would you?"

"Yeah, I suppose. But still . . ."

"You can't blame them, then."

"I can too," said the praying mantis. "It's not fair! Nobody wants to be my friend."

"Maybe another praying mantis?"

"Oh, that's no good. We eat one another as well."

Hector shuddered and looked over his

shoulder. Behind him was the stream. In front was the praying mantis with her skinny legs and sharp chin. "You don't eat wumblebugs, do you?"

The praying mantis peered at him with enormous eyes. "Never eat red bugs. Nasty." For an instant she grew perfectly still, balancing carefully on her back four legs. Then she sprang out, folded her jagged front legs around a small moth, and was back, crunching. "Let's face it—no one wants to be my friend. I gave a party. Did they come? No."

"Oh," said Hector, still recovering from the attack on the moth.

"Then they had a party and didn't even invite me. See what I mean?"

"Maybe if you did something nice. Like for instance—"

"Oh, who cares? I don't want to be part of their stupid club anyway. They're just a bunch of big bullies."

"Seems to me," said Hector, "that you're a lot bigger than—"

"What do you know? You're just as bad. You're mean and you're red and you taste bad too."

Hector scratched his nose. "Sorry you feel that way. Still, could you tell me which fork leads to the meadow?"

"Why should I?"

"My friend went on ahead, and I need to find him."

The praying mantis gulped down the last of the moth. "What kind of friend? Anything good to eat?"

"Why, he's a l . . . l . . . like me. Red. Nasty, like you say."

"Then go find him yourself. That roly-poly must be here someplace. Like I always say—if you can't join 'em, eat 'em!"

The praying mantis cackled at her own joke and disappeared down the roly-poly's trail.

Chapter Eight

The Meadow

Hector squinted up the two branches of the stream. They both looked the same. There was no trace of Lance.

An orange butterfly circled over Hector's head, then fluttered up the left branch. Hector followed for a few steps and stopped. Was that a song drifting down the stream? He swiveled his antennae to hear. Then he started to run.

Lance sat whistling at the edge of the water. "Hey," he said. "What took you so long?"

"Never mind." Hector looked at his friend. He took a deep breath. "The bugs here aren't very friendly. Let's go."

With their heads down and antennae straight ahead, Hector and Lance climbed the steep, hot trail. Once in a while they heard a deep rumble of thunder and looked up, expecting rain. The clouds pressed down, thick and gray.

Sometime after noon they heard the bubbling song of a meadowlark perched on the edge of a wide field. Bees flew everywhere, rushing to finish their work before the storm.

Lance flew up to a sunflower and looked around. "This is more like it. Hear that katydid song? Cool, huh?"

The whole place vibrated with sound. *Whirrrrrrrrrrrrrrr* . . . A deep chorus came from the grasshoppers as they rubbed their wings and legs together. *HmmmRmmmmm* . . . A fly swooped and sped away. *Tick-tick-buzz* . . . That must be the katydid.

"Hey, wait!" Hector called as Lance spread his wings and flew ahead. *Crunch-crunch-crunch-crunch.* A long line of ants blocked his path. Their feet stomped in rhythm together. Each carried a bundle of food, and they all looked straight ahead.

"Hello there," said Hector. "Would you mind if I just . . ."

The ants marched on, chanting under their breath. Hector took a running jump over them and crashed midair into a bright green bug with horns.

"Ouch!" cried Hector.

"Buzzzz offff!" came the green bug's voice as it passed.

"Wow," said Lance. "A treehopper! And there's a leafhopper behind you!"

"Aah!" Hector yelled as an orange-and-blue-striped insect leaped over his head. "Too many hoppers around here."

"And look at the aphids," said Lance. "Crunchy on the outside, sweet and juicy in the middle. Yum!"

Hector watched him grab a small, wingless bug that was sucking on a leaf. Then, across the meadow, he saw a small figure coming to meet them. It was Uncle Baxter.

The old wumblebug was missing a leg. His exoskeleton—the outer coating that protects a bug—was dented as if from a great battle. As he came closer Hector saw that he leaned on a wooden cane polished with the wax of bees.

Uncle Baxter squinted and spoke in a gruff voice. "So, you've come. Good. Let's get to work." He turned and limped away.

"Uncle Baxter," said Hector. "This is my friend Lance."

"This is family business, Hector," Uncle Baxter answered over his shoulder. "The lacewing can wait out here."

Hector ducked as a katydid came in for a landing. "Lance, I'll go and talk to him, okay? Then I'll come back."

"No problem," said Lance. He was watching the katydids fight over the best singing spot in the grass. "I'll be right here."

Chapter Nine

Uncle Baxter's Bees

Uncle Baxter moved quickly in spite of the cane. "We've got a lot to see, so keep your eyes open. Fourteen hives, all full this time of year."

Hector hurried alongside. "You must be eating lots of honey!"

"Eat it? Don't be ridiculous. I just sell it."

"But how do you control the bees?"

"Ah, there's the question." Uncle Baxter waved his cane but did not slow down. "It's all about the queens. Each hive has a queen, and that queen rules over fifty or sixty thousand workers. And who do you think rules the queens, eh? That's right—me!"

"Is that how you . . . you lost your leg?"

"It was worth it!" The glint in Uncle Baxter's eyes sent a shiver down Hector's antennae. "I have some stories—some secrets—that no one knows."

"Like what?"

"So you want to know, do you? Very good. What makes a queen bee, do you think? Hmm? Royal jelly! A great secret of life. When the hive is crowded, it is fed to a few of the young."

"And then what?" asked Hector.

"They hatch as queens. But only one can rule, and they fight to the death to decide. At that moment I am there waiting, ready to choose the strongest. I join with her as she fights each of her sisters. Battle after battle. Two against one. And that queen always believes it was I—I who gave her power!"

"So then she does what you want?"

"Exactly. She gives me her honey. Royal jelly as well. Over the years I've come to rule all the hives this way. I've had my share of injuries, but the jelly keeps me strong. Come, you'll see for yourself."

Uncle Baxter led the way through fields of star thistle and clover. Against the woods stood the hives in the hollow stumps of trees.

The buzzing grew to a deep roar. Black-and-gold bees zoomed past Hector's head and between his antennae, making trips to the meadow and back. At the entrance to the hives they wiggled and waggled, telling one another the best spots for nectar. Hector couldn't understand a thing.

Uncle Baxter stopped at the largest hive. "You'll need this," he said, and rubbed Hector with some pollen that smelled like the beehive. The guard bees did not look up as Uncle Baxter hobbled in toward a bee that was longer and thinner than the rest.

Hector stood in the entrance, smelling hot honey and wax. Workers hurried everywhere, building row after row of little wax rooms and feeding the babies inside. Hector took a step, then another, along the waxy edge of the honeycomb.

One of the rooms was full of honey, golden

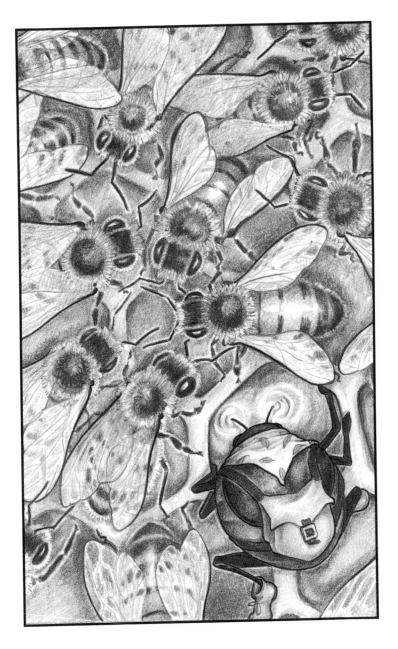

and deep. Hector leaned over for a taste. It was very sweet. He leaned farther and slipped in, up to his knees in honey. He kicked and slid deeper—up to his belly, up to his back. He grabbed the wax wall, but it broke and he tumbled backward, with his legs in the air.

"Help!" Hector cried. Honey caught his wings, and his words drowned in the roar of the buzzing hive.

Chapter Ten

Sticky Swimming

Hector squirmed and twisted and tried to roll over, but the honey held him tight. He waved his legs, searching for something to grab, some way to pull himself up. He yelled for his uncle over and over. He tried to thrash his wings, but he could not move them at all.

He was trapped.

Hector lay still and tried to think. If he wiggled, he sank faster. Better to spread out. Don't hurry. Don't move. What did someone say? Haste makes waste.

The honey gurgled up to his face. Maybe he could eat his way out. He took a taste, then another. He burped. The honey was starting to taste bad.

Maybe a bee would notice him. After all, they would not want wumblebugs floating around in their food.

The honey was thick and warm. Hector sank deeper until only his feet stuck out.

At first everything was golden under the honey. Then everything went black.

"It's him," called a distant voice. "Get him outside, girls."

Hector opened his eyes. He was upside down, attached by his six legs to six bees flying through the air. They plopped him down in front of the hive and flew off.

Uncle Baxter stood over him, frowning and tapping his cane. "Well? What have you got to say for yourself?"

Hector lay still for a moment, breathing the open air. He sat up and wiped honey off his face. He felt a little sick.

"I'm sorry. I slipped, and then—"

"Of all the stupid things . . ." Uncle Baxter turned to watch the last bees fly into the hive as the wind blew spits of rain. "Eh, never mind. At

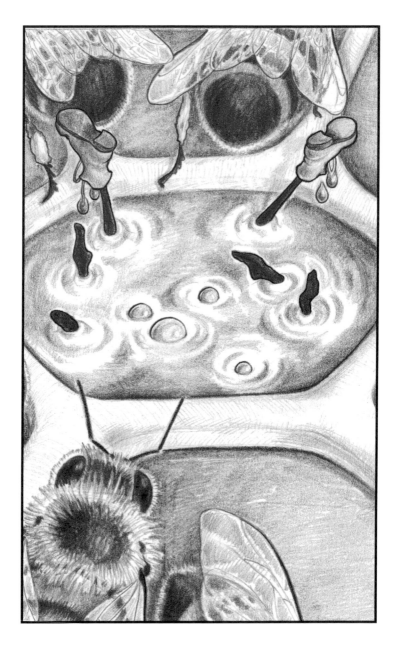

least we'll get some rain. A dry summer like this, you've got to keep an eye on the bees. They'll steal the honey back."

"Doesn't it belong to them?" Hector scrambled to his feet.

"They're working for me, right? Remember—always take as much honey as you can. Keep them busy and they'll do as they're told."

They began to walk to the high corner of the meadow, where Uncle Baxter had carved his home. "How do you sell it?" asked Hector. "Do bugs come and pick it up?"

Uncle Baxter shook his head. "You can't have neighbors if you're running a bee farm. Can't crowd the bees. Tomorrow I'll show you the packing rooms under my hole. That's where I need help."

"I'd better get Lance indoors," said Hector. "Looks like a big storm."

Uncle Baxter stopped and stared at him. "Do you think I'd have a lacewing in my hole? Whatever for?"

"Lance is my friend," said Hector. "He came

all this way with me. He's a great cook, too. We could make—"

"A cook? Bah. Food is greatly overestimated. Now, you work hard, and these hives can be yours someday. You've no need for lacewings."

With a swing of his cane, Uncle Baxter led the way down a tunnel to a small sleeping room, waved in the direction of the food cave, and left Hector alone in the great wumblebug hole built on honey.

Chapter Eleven

The Maze

Hector fell across the bed. The day had been long—hiking up the stream, following his uncle. The beehive. He needed a moment to rest. Then he would go find Lance.

He stretched out and closed his eyes.

Kaboom!

Hector woke to a crash of thunder as the clouds sent rain pouring into the night.

He sat up, unsure where he was. His legs were stiff and his wings were still sticky with honey. Then he remembered. His uncle's farm. The meadow. The next instant he knew that something was terribly wrong—Lance was out in the storm alone!

Grabbing his pack, Hector felt his way out the

door. The tunnels to either side were dark. Hector looked harder. From one side came a faint glow of light, barely enough to see.

He threw himself down the corridor, following his feet as they fell on the packed dirt. The light shifted and grew dim. Was he going uphill or down? Right or left? He ran on, tunnel after tunnel, turning corners as he saw lights flicker ahead. He heard a door closing and the distant buzz of bees.

Hector followed the sound, past room after room piled with boxes and jars. Uncle Baxter's packing rooms. Yellow candles flickered and threw long shadows down the halls. Dark shapes of bees disappeared ahead.

"Wait!" called Hector. "I need to get out! Which way is out?"

One of the bees peeled off to the side. Hector followed and found himself at a dead end. The air was stuffy with the sweet smell of burning beeswax. There was a single bee, reaching to snuff out the candle.

"Don't!" said Hector.

"Save wax. That's the rule," said the bee.

"Please, can you show me which way leads up to the meadow?"

"Too busy. Must work. On time. My job."

"Please, it's important. I've got to find my friend."

"All friend. No friend. Smell the same."

"No, this one is different. He's up in the meadow, and I need to find him."

"Not different. Pack honey. Stick label. Stack jars. Box up. Ship out. Save wax." The bee put out the candle and scuttled away.

Hector felt his way in the dark, stumbling over boxes. The walls were smooth except for one rectangle of wood—a door. An old door that was stuck. Hector pulled and tugged until it opened, creaking on its hinges.

The tunnel beyond was narrow and rough. Hector could feel that it sloped up and was just wide enough to squeeze through. He began to climb, pushing dirt behind him, hoping to break through.

The tunnel narrowed. Hector's digging

slowed. The tunnel closed in and stopped.

Hector stopped too. He took a step backward, then another. Then he heard a terrible sound—a thud as the tunnel behind him collapsed.

The only way out was up. Hector put his head down and dug for his life. Moving up, always up, he groped with his front legs. Another thud, right behind him this time. He scraped and scratched and struggled to breathe.

His antennae caught the smell of air.

Fresh, wet air. Not too far away.

He dug faster as he reached the last layer of dirt. *Thlop*—a pile of dirt buried his back legs. He pulled himself out and tumbled forward into a door. He pushed it open and stepped out into the furious wind of the storm.

Chapter Twelve

Thunder and Lightning

Hector tightened his pack. Inside it he could feel the smooth pebble that the termite lady had given him for luck.

He would need all the luck he could get. The sky battered him with great, plopping drops. A blast of wet air tried to blow him off course. Hector put his nose to the wind and kept going, step by step. He called for Lance and wished he had never fallen asleep.

Lance was right where they had parted hours ago. He was drenched and shivering in a puddle of water. He was much too cold to fly.

Without a word Hector pulled his friend to a dry spot between some rocks. He opened his pack and handed Lance a mint leaf to cheer him up.

"I'm sorry," Hector said. "I should never have left you out here. Uncle Baxter was showing me around, telling me stories—stuff you can't believe! Then I fell asleep. . . ."

"You know," said Lance as he chewed, "this whole trip has been great."

"Are you kidding? You could have drowned out here!"

"But I didn't—thanks to you. You're the best, Hector. First you saved me at the whirligig pool . . ."

"You saved me back," said Hector. "Plus you offered to come in the first place."

"I wanted to come," said Lance. "So that doesn't count. Then you made that shelter for me by the stream because of the lightning."

"Yeah, and you found the honeysuckle for breakfast. That was good."

"It was, huh. But then you brought me here to this meadow, which is so great. The music, the food . . ."

"You can have it," said Hector. "I'd rather be home."

"The point is, what are friends for? To help each other. So you did all these things for me, and now it's my turn." Lance shook the rain from his dripping wings. "I've been wondering—is this place really for you? You don't even like bees."

Hector rubbed his forehead. "I don't know. Since I got here, nothing's gone right. In the beehive I fell in the honey—don't laugh, it was horrible—and then I got lost in the packing rooms. No, I don't like it here. But I'm stuck."

"Don't think that way. You have to stand up to your uncle. You have to tell him to find somebody else. I'll help. It'll take two of us to talk to a guy like that."

"That's for sure," said Hector. "Only . . ."

"Only what?"

"I'd be letting him down. You know, he's not all that old or tired. Maybe he just needs someone to hear his stories. Somebody besides a bee."

Lance sighed. "That's true. I didn't think of it that way."

"I can't leave, and I don't want to stay," said Hector. "And I'm not the right bug for the job."

He lay down and tried to sleep. The storm blew, and the rocks were bumpy and hard. It would be a long night, but at least he had a friend nearby.

Chapter Thirteen

The Rescue

The meadowlark woke Hector and Lance with a song about the morning's clear skies. A few bees made early trips out of the hives, and a magpie darted about, searching for the shiny bits and pieces that magpies love to find.

Hector rose and stretched. Across the soggy meadow came his uncle, limping with every step.

Uncle Baxter frowned at the two young bugs. "What in blazes are you doing out here in a storm? Even bees have more sense!"

Hector felt his antennae get hot. "Lance was out here. You might not understand, but I had to find him. He's my friend."

"Of course I understand!" Uncle Baxter

waved his cane as if to brush away Hector's words. The magpie followed every move of the glittering stick. "I've got plenty of friends—all my bees working here for me!"

"Friendship's not about that." Now Hector was so angry he could hardly breathe. "It's about enjoying somebody, being happy when he's happy. And when he's sad, trying to help. You have no friends. And what's more—there's no way I'd stay here. Life is more than making honey!"

"Friends come and go," said Uncle Baxter with a frown. "They let you down. At some point you can only depend on yourself."

"Lance has never let me down. Not once!" A thought flashed into Hector's mind. "And if you were smart, you'd realize it's not me you need here. If you were smart, you'd see that it's Lance who likes the meadow."

"Don't be ridiculous!" Uncle Baxter shook his cane over his head. "A lacewing in my—"

At that moment the magpie made her move. Swooping down from the branch, she plucked

Uncle Baxter up in her long black beak and headed for the sky.

In an instant Lance was in the air. He zoomed up to the magpie and dived again and again at her beady eyes. He followed her in a crazy zigzag over the meadow. Over the hives. Over the great wumblebug hole. Over the damp clover far below. He dived and poked until the magpie dropped her tiny treasure and flew away.

Hector's wits returned just in time. Joining Lance in the air, he flapped with all his might to break his uncle's fall, and the three bugs landed in a heap.

"Why the devil did it do that? Birds don't eat wumblebugs!" sputtered Uncle Baxter. He had lost his cane, and his five legs were tangled up.

"She collects things." Lance was panting. "She must have seen that shiny cane."

Uncle Baxter stared at Lance as if he were seeing a ghost. "But why did you fly after her?"

Lance looked surprised. "You're Hector's uncle, that's why. And Hector is my best friend."

Uncle Baxter turned away and looked out over

the soggy meadow. He was silent for a long time.

Hector and Lance looked at each other and shrugged. Finally Lance opened the tattered pack and pulled out a mushy glob that had once been a blueberry.

"Would you like some berries, Mr. Baxter?"

Uncle Baxter turned back to them and smiled. He had not smiled in a long time, and his pointy face twisted in all directions. "You boys come in," he said. "Come in the hole and get dry; have something to eat before you go."

"You know," said Hector, "we could help you out. During the busy season, that is—we could come back up and help you when you need us."

His uncle looked at him and then at Lance. "I'd like that. You come back later in the summer. Bring your friend here . . . bring Lance when you come. You're a fortunate bug, Hector, to have a friend like that."

And they walked together back to the great, empty wumblebug hole as the air all around them filled again with bees.

Chapter Fourteen

Welcome and Good-bye

Hector and Lance were too tired to leave that morning or that afternoon. While Uncle Baxter worked, they rested and ate, and then went to sleep early.

By the time Hector stumbled out of bed, sunlight was already pouring through the high windows. The smell of cooking drifted down the hall.

In the kitchen was Uncle Baxter, dressed in an apron and squeezing a blackberry. Lance stood over the stove, breaking snail eggs into a hot pan. "Just in time," he said. "We're having omelettes, honey cakes . . ."

"Fresh juice . . . ," said Uncle Baxter.

"And parsley on the side. Take a seat!" Lance slid a huge plate under Hector's nose.

Uncle Baxter leaned back and watched him eat. "Well, your friend here knows how to cook."

"I know," said Hector with his mouth full. "Wow, I've never tasted cakes like these. How long have you been up?"

"Hours," said Lance. "We've been all around the farm. Top to bottom."

"And he's showing me how to cook! Who says you can't teach an old bug some new tricks?" Uncle Baxter chuckled and tucked some hollow sticks filled with honey into Hector's pack. Then he nodded at Lance. "I think she'll be ready now."

"Who's ready?" asked Hector.

"C'mon," said Lance, pulling him to the door as Uncle Baxter stomped on ahead with his new cane, a dark brown twig. "He's giving us a bee swarm to take home. Isn't that great?"

"Now, wait a minute. If you think I'm going to—"

"Don't worry. I'll take care of them," said Lance. "You know, bees are good for a garden. They spread pollen, so there's more fruit. Plus you can use the honey to kill germs if you get a cut. Isn't that amazing?"

Hector laughed. "You sound like a bee farmer."

"You boys ready?" called Uncle Baxter. "We'll let them loose."

He thumped on the ground with his cane. A stream of bees flooded out of the hive. They followed their queen, and their queen followed Hector and Lance across the meadow and away.

Chapter Fifteen

All That Glitters

The journey was much faster downhill. Rainwater splashed and filled the rocky places that had been dry. Green growing things poked up along the banks. Behind Hector and Lance came the cloud of bees, searching and sniffing and flying everywhere like bits of sun.

Late in the morning Hector saw a leaf bobbing down the streambed in front of them. It was the termite lady. Her umbrella still sparkled with rain.

"Hello!" called Hector. "How was your trip?"

The termite lady turned to watch them catch up. "A grandmother's work is never done!" she said. "But as I always say, don't wear out your welcome! Time flies, and it's time to go home.

After all, a rolling stone gathers no moss!"

"No," said Hector. "Anyway, this is the friend I told you about. He's going to help out at the bee farm when we come back."

"Make new friends, but keep the old," she said, smiling at Lance. "To each his own! All that glitters is not gold!"

Lance smiled back.

Hector reached in his pack and pulled the honey sticks out. "A gift," he said with a bow. "From Baxter's Bee Farm. As you might say, the best things in life are free."

The termite lady's eyes grew wide. "My goodness, what will they think of next? Well, live and learn, young bugs. All's well that ends well!"

She waved good-bye, and Hector and Lance started off again. But when Hector looked back, she was still standing there, sipping from the stick. "Look," he said to Lance. "She likes it."

The two friends laughed and jumped from rock to rock, slipping and sliding down through the cool, rushing water all the way home.

Elizabeth Shreeve grew up in a family of writers and scientists who taught her to chase butterflies and otherwise scare the daylights out of small creatures in the local marshes and fields. She also liked to read and would have become a librarian if books could be stored outdoors. A graduate of Harvard College and the Harvard Graduate School of Design, she balances a career in environmental design with writing stories and reading in silly voices to her husband and sons. The origin of Hector Fuller's name and species is a closely-held family secret that Elizabeth is happy to share at book signings and school visits, where she talks with children about the natural world, the life of a writer, and the joys of becoming a lifelong reader.

Don't miss any of the Stink Squad's scentsational adventures!

The Malodorous Mess

The Stink Squad must stop what smells like an evil plot to rule the world!

The Reek from Outer Space

Something strange is in the air—and it's not from this world. . . .

The African Sniffari

There won't be any time to relax and smell the aromas on this sticky vacation.

The Fume in the Tomb

The Stink Squad has to find a precious artifact before an angry mummy finds them!

By Katherine Pebley O'Neal • Illustrated by Daryll Collins

Aladdin Paperbacks • Simon & Schuster • Children's Publishing Division
www.SimonSaysKids.com